The Journal Of My Journey

Shaena Queen Jones

A teenage love Story

Queen J

ENTEGRITY
CHOICE PUBLISHING

Personal Reflections

May God's command continue to be a light unto my path. Thank you, God, for bringing me to the point of a personal revelation of who you are and what you desire of my life.

Thank you for the personal journey in the last two years. Thank you for preparing me slowly for the publication of this work that you will use to give to the world.

Thank you that the girl this book has been written for receives it with no extra struggle to the person she receives it from. Bless those who will read this story and come away with a refreshed outlook on life, help them to know that change is possible and inevitable if they seek it. Most of all, thank you for gifting me with the gift of writing.
Dated: July 16, 2016

It has not been easy to write my story and regurgitate the hurt and pain. I am grateful that God has made it possible by being my peace through this entire journey.
Dated: October 10th 2016

Here I am sitting on my bed with my laptop on my lap getting this book ready for publication. The one thing that has stuck with me through all this is, "Never give up on what you truly want and always believe in yourself. Sometimes it takes longer than expected, but in the end, it will be worth it. I'm doing this one for me, and *all* my babies."

Happy 26th birthday, Shaena
Dated: December 19, 2016

A Special Thank You To
Corey-DeVon

You have played an amazing part in my story, "The Journal of My Journey." From my very first job until our move to Atlanta, you were right there listening when I first told you about this book. Grateful that you always remind me that my faith is out of this world. Well, here goes nothing; I release my faith and let this book go into the world.

Thank you for your unwavering support on my endeavors. I will always believe in you and know whatever you set your mind to do, you will accomplish it.

Foreword

"The Journal of My Journey" by my best friend and sister in Christ, Queen J. You have made an awesome choice! You are not only getting ready to read a story about someone's life, but this book will also help you start and embrace your own journey.

First off, I must say that I am very proud of this young lady. She is not only publishing her book, but she is following her purpose to help others achieve their goals. Although this book may be directed towards young women, this is a must read for everyone!

Every life journey is mixed with both bad and good times. Life is indeed what you make of it. It takes a real soldier to endure storms. As you read this book, you will read a story that will make you cry, smile, and think.

The words to the song, "If I Can Help Somebody" is a life goal for Queen J.

"If I can help somebody, as I pass along,
If I can cheer somebody, with a word or song,
If I can show somebody, that he's traveling wrong,
Then my living shall not be in vain."

It's one thing for Queen J to tell a story about life, but for her to share her story to help others and encourage them to hold on and be strong shows how possible a breakthrough can be in the lives of others.

In this book, you will read about her struggles in life and how she dealt with them. She does not simply tell us of her pain, but she shows us how to use pain as a springboard to success. Her testimony will give you hope on how to weather all kinds of ups and downs in life, and come out standing tall. You will see her Faith in action and the hard work that has propelled Queen J to her destiny.

If you are a single mother, struggling with life, *this book is for you!*

If you are a young woman who is lost and confused about life, *this book is for you!*

Fellas, if you have a friend, sister, or daughter, give them this book. Likewise, fellas, *this book is for you!*

I thank God for the opportunity to witness Queen J share her life story with the world. The Lord has brought her from a mighty long way. This not only shows how good God has been to her but it also shows that all ups and downs are temporary!

This book will summon you to reflect on your own life. You will be motivated to get up and take a stand. Don't worry about your past, press forward. Don't worry about your mistakes and problems, they do not define you.

I pray you are ready to go on a journey with Queen J as you read "The Journal of My Journey."

Bertram "Be'Jay" Major
Best Friend and Brother in Christ

From My Heart to Yours

First and foremost, thank you for purchasing this book. I am so very delighted to have the opportunity to share my message with you. Thank you for the real investment, your time. Time is one of our most valuable assets; you can never get back time. Let me assure you, this book is a true investment into the life of a young Queen.

It is my truest intent to be as honest as possible about the events that have taken place in my life. Take my lessons learned to transform the lives of young queens all around the world.

Shaena Jones
"Changing lives one book at a time."

Dedication

This book is dedicated to Ms. Clark.

As I am coming to the end of this project, I have thought so many times what I've wanted to say and how I've felt about this entire process. Seeing you last night was God's confirmation to me that I am doing exactly what He says to do.

I am so glad I was able to share with you about my book and give you a hug. You inspired my first book in the 12th grade. I received the highest average in education between 2008 and 2009. I never realized how that achievement tied in with where I was headed in life. All I can say is thank you. You were an amazing supportive teacher and for this I am forever grateful to you for believing in me.

Preface

On December 24, 1990, at 8:33 a.m., a woman gave birth to a beautiful baby girl. Four days later, she was given away to the Georgia Department of Family and Children Services.

As the young girl grew, her desire to understand life became clear. Taking trips back and forth between two families left the young girl a tad confused. She was taught that her biological family lived one place, whereas the family she had grown to know and love was back home awaiting her return. The older the girl became, the harder life became. She found it hard to deal with life. By age 16, she was diagnosed with depression.

One could ask how is it likely for a child not to have separation issues or a smidgen bit of confusion with so much going on in their life. The girl sought to get a clearer understanding about her life and began to search for answers.

After spending sleepless nights praying for an understanding and crying tears on her pillow, the young girl couldn't understand why she wasn't living with her family. She wanted her biological parents to love her so bad. Her need to feel her biological father's embrace left the young girl wanting attention. She set out on a quest to find someone who would love her as much as she wanted to be loved. The young girl's insecurities, lack of self-love, and self-respect were evident.

The young girl turned to the one thing that could help her cope, sex, men, and finding love at a very early age. Every time the young girl invested her time into a person, it's as if they played on her weakness; what a mistake. Her misunderstanding led her into some dark places that her mind couldn't keep her. The lack of stability from the biological father had caused the girl to turn to guys who reflected him. The girl wanted to be loved, accepted, and needed because she had spent her entire life as an outsider struggling to fit in. She didn't know what self-love was. She was consumed with trying to analyze why her biological parents didn't want her around.

Six years later, the girl in this story is finally healing from her past. She has two beautiful children, and is on a path to truly loving herself -- that young girl is me!

Ms. Shaena Jones
Queen J
Mother-Conqueror-Motivational Speaker-Entrepreneur-Author

Contents

Personal Reflections...III

A Special Thank You.. V

Foreword...VII

From My Heart to Yours IX

Preface...XIII

Introduction.. XVII

Chapter 1
Bullies, Cheetah Girls, Losing Friends *(7th Grade)* 19

Chapter 2
Bullying Continues, First Crush, High School Decisions *(8th Grade)* 23

Chapter 3
Freshman, Hurt & Suicide *(9th Grade)*.................................. 27

Chapter 4
Soccer and Reality Checks *(10th Grade)* 31

Chapter 5
Life Turns Upside Down *(11th Grade)*...................................... 33

Chapter 6
A Role Model - Coach Tolbert... 41

Chapter 7
Senior Year: Pregnancy And Rejection *(12th Grade)* 43

Chapter 8
Graduation 2009 49

Chapter 9
Letters That Explain It All 53

Personal Reflections Workbook 57

Introduction

At one point in my life, I was the girl who was in church every Sunday. I was in everything possible: dance, choir, and even played roles in skits (including a tree). I was always picked to do a welcome, or I was volunteering to say the prayer.

Things quickly changed when I was introduced to another life because the pain inside me was causing me so much confusion. Now that I am older and healing from my childhood, I have thought about the things that could have made a difference in my life.

In doing so, I have chosen to bring you "The Journal of My Journey." Join me as I venture on a quest to share with you my story about how the confusion and lack of self-love caused me to spiral down the wrong path at a very young age.

I was blinded by pain and believed that I was making all of the right decisions. I had no one to run to for support. This book is intended to inspire you to think about your life and understand that life goes on beyond where you are.

I want to help you grow as a young Queen, but only if you are willing and ready. I have experienced so many obstacles throughout my teen years, and I am thankful to have this chance to minister to you beautiful, young Queens.

 I have a new path for my future generations. Come with me and see my journey. Most of all, come with me and grow into that beautiful bumble bee which you are destined to be.

It is my prayer that this book not only changes your life in a positive and powerful way, but it also inspires you to be so much more than you were before you read it.

"Now that I have learned, I can teach."
Shaena

"Float like a butterfly Sting Like a bee"
Muhammad Ali

1

Bullies, Cheetah Girls, Losing Friends

7th Grade

"Big foot, four eyes, Shaq," they chatted in my direction. I seemed to always be a target; it never got old. I was the one everyone seemedto want to pick on and nag. Being that I was taller than most of my classmates, I guess I understood.

Walking through the halls of Glenn Hills Middle School was such a dread, I hated it. Math was my hardest subject. I just couldn't understand it and thought that this might be the first year that I would be kept back. Social Studies and Language Arts were the two subjects that I loved. The favorite of them all was Art. I kept trying to find an outlet. I didn't want to be a target, but I was too afraid of standing up for myself because I never wanted to fight.

One day I went home from school crying and told my mother that the kids at school were always talking about me and calling me big foot. She said, "Shaena, those kids are just jealous of you." That wasn't a good enough answer for me and it dang sure didn't solve the issue of being bullied. Why would anyone be jealous of me? I didn't have designer clothes, I wore those white K Swiss, and I was friendly as ever. I just didn't get it. I thought to myself, "Why can't I just fit in?" My 7th grade was the year I started to lose myself. I really thought I was ugly. Besides, the world was telling me that I wasn't good enough, I was nothing.

My friends Lashaun and Christine were my favorite people in school. Christine and I were friends in the 6th grade, and Lashaun and I met in the 7th grade. We were all super close. The movie, "Cheetah Girls," came out that year. The movie was about these girls who came from different backgrounds and formed a singing group. We thought for sure we were the Cheetah Girls. I even wrote letters to the group; they were amazing friends! Cheetah Girls were the best! One song says, "We are sisters, we stand together, we make up one big family. Though we don't look the same, our stripes are different, different colors…" I truly believed that we were sisters and we were unbreakable.

One day someone started a rumor saying that I said something negative about Christine. Honestly, I don't remember saying anything about Christine. Christine was furious when she heard the rumor. She confronted me and asked if I said it, but I didn't. Cindy, one of my other friends, swore I said something negative about Christine.

Suddenly out of nowhere Christine stopped speaking to me. It hurt that we weren't speaking after all the fun we had and the secrets we shared. I couldn't accept that our friendship was over. Soon I found out that Christine was going to be moving to Washington, DC. I was devastated because she was my friend and it hurt me to know my friend was not speaking to me and she was about to live far away. I thought I would never hear from her again. And just like that, the Cheetah Girls were over. My friendship was gone out the window. Even Lashaun became distant after the conflict. I couldn't understand why it happened so abruptly; I was alone again.

In chorus, I met Olivia. She was very nice and we both sang together. She became one of my close friends. We were always out at concerts sitting together singing. Me and Olivia became closer and closer as the year went on. We built an unbreakable bond that no one could change. Olivia was a really good friend and the plus was that she was smart and always encouraging me to stay focused on the right things. It hurt that we weren't speaking after all the fun we had and the secrets we shared. I couldn't accept that our friendship was over.

By the time the year ended, I barely made it through my math class with a passing grade. I was ready for summer, and looked forward to being out of school because I was tired of the bullying and hearing about how big my feet were. On the last day of school, the teachers said goodbye and enjoy your summer. When the last bell rang, I hopped on my bus and sank into my seat ready to get home.

Bullying is never okay. To bully means to use superior strength or influence to intimidate. When you see someone who's different from you, don't nag, pick, or be mean towards them. You never know what's going on with someone or how they may feel about being bullied. Besides, no one really likes mean ole bullies anyway.

Imagine if someone were bullying you, how would you feel?

____

____

____

If you're being bullied who is someone you can talk to about it?

____

____

____

Please, if you witness someone being bullied, speak up and speak out!

2

Bullying Continues, First Crush, High School Decisions

8th Grade

After the summer was over, the 8th grade began. I was determined that my last year at Glenn Hills Middle School would be the best year ever. Eighth grade got off to a great start. I joined so many clubs, took many exciting field trips, and had so much fun. The bullying never ceased, but for some strange reason, it didn't bother me as much as it did previously. I became a peer mediator and was excited to help my peers resolve conflict without becoming physical.

Next year I would be moving on to high school, and I had a very big decision to make. After touring my new zone school, Glenn Hills High School, I was afraid to walk the halls of that school. As weeks went by, there were a few school announcements about a magnet high school. The magnet school, A. R. Johnson, was a health, science, and engineering school so it caught my attention.

One day I decided to go by my Guidance Counselor's office and picked up an application to A. R. Johnson High School. I was tired of being bullied, and I knew if I went to Glenn Hills High School, things could only get worse. I went home and announced to my parents my plans to attend A. R. Johnson High School. My parents were so proud of me, but little did they know, it had nothing to do with the school and academics but everything to do with how I was feeling inside.

When testing day came for A. R. Johnson High School, I was a nervous wreck. I sat at my desk looking at the test questions as if I was reading a foreign language. I just knew I was going to fail the test. The questions on the test were extremely hard. When we finished the test, we were instructed to walk through the halls and tour the school. There were a lot of prospective students taking the test. A few familiar faces were in the crowd, and there were some students I had never seen in my life. As we were disbursing from the school, some of the students stated that the test was a bit challenging, confirming my opinion. We had to wait 4-8 weeks before we knew our test scores.

For now, eighth grade was going smoothly. There was this boy in my class named Rodriguez, who I thought was so handsome. He was tall like me, so I thought we would be the perfect pair; I liked him. I can't believe I was bold enough to admit I liked someone. Everyone in class knew I liked him, and they always talked negative about him, but I always stood up for him and defended him (funny how I never stood up for myself).

When we were at school, Rodriguez never really talked to me that much, but I didn't care because sometimes we would talk on the phone after school. Even though I told Rodriguez I liked him, he never liked me, and I couldn't understand why. Subsequently, he ended up getting a girlfriend, and I cried every night. I was so hurt. I often asked myself, "Why wasn't I his girlfriend? Why doesn't he like me?" I liked him and never understand the rejection. Soon, I begin to get over the crush I had for Rodriguez.

Before eighth grade was over, another boy had my attention. His name was Mark. I got his number right before summer began, and we started to talk. Mark ended up becoming my first boyfriend. I was excited that finally someone wanted me. I did everything possible to keep him. I spent my allowance on him, buying him whatever he needed. I never cared what anyone thought about how I was spending my money. It was my money and I could spend it any way I chose. According to Momma and Daddy, I wasn't allowed to have a boyfriend. I didn't care about their boyfriend rule; I sneaked out of the house often to meet Mark at his house.

One day Mark and I were at his parents' home alone. He asked me to "do it" with him. I was a little nervous but agreed, so we did it. It was my first time having sex. After it was over, I felt weird. I walked home and never felt like I was the same girl ever again. My life started to change. I became very clingy to Mark, and he began to become very distant. I couldn't understand why.

One thought I did have as to why Mark was distant is that I didn't know much about sex. My mom never talked to me about sex and boys. All I knew about sex was what Mark told me and what I knew from my peers. In my sex education class, I learned a little about sex. Truth be told, I only "did it" because he was my first boyfriend and I was afraid to lose him. Even so, sex could not stop us from drifting apart. I never mentioned anything to Mark about what I was feeling because I didn't want to give him a reason to even think of leaving me. Besides, he was the first person that ever really wanted me and I wasn't about to let him go.

One day while I was checking the mail, there was a letter addressed to the parents of Shaena A. Jones from A. R. Johnson High School. I was anxious to know what was inside of the letter so I asked Mom if I could open it. The letter stated, "We are proud to inform you that your child, Shaena A. Jones, has been accepted to attend A. R. Johnson Health Science Engineering High School for the upcoming school year for the Health Science track. I jumped up and down with excitement. No more zone school for me, I was going to A. R. Johnson High School! I called Mark to tell him the news. He was happy for me but still very distant. Getting ready for high school had to be the longest summer ever. Between having my first boyfriend, doing it for the first time, and being accepted to A. R. Johnson High School, I felt myself changing. I wasn't the same Shaena anymore.

One thing I do wish is that my mom would have had a long conversation with me about sex and boys. I did not understand that at age 15, sex can wait; if a boy likes you, he will wait for you. What I have come to know is that you should never allow a boy to tell you that if you love him you should be having sex. If he loves you, he will respect your decision and wait.

I advise any teenager contemplating sex to talk with a parent, aunt, teacher, family member, friends, etc., about your feelings. Never be afraid to talk to someone about sex.

Parents, sex is a very important topic. Take the time to talk to your children, especially your daughters. Take the time to explain to your children the importance of waiting and why it matters. Parents and other adults can Google "sex."

3

Freshman, Hurt & Suicide

9th Grade

As my freshman year began, I tried very hard to hold onto my relationship with Mark. He was still distant, and I couldn't figure out what more to say to keep us going. I constantly reminded him of how much I loved him and that I would do anything to be with him. I wanted him to tell me what had changed. Out of nowhere, he started being mean.

Mark was a student at my zone school, Glenn Hills High school. He rode the bus with me in the morning to his school, and when I arrived at his school, I caught a different bus to get to A. R. Johnson High School.

One day I purposely missed the bus and stayed behind to see Mark. When he saw me, he took off, walking superfast, as if he didn't even see me. I stood watching him and felt empty. As I walked to the office to have another bus called to get me to my school, I couldn't help but feel lost. I arrived at school that day feeling rejected, a feeling I knew all too well. It was at this point that I began writing. I released all of my feelings and thoughts onto paper.

At school, my grades suffered. My parents signed me up for the after-school program because of my grades. It wasn't long before I started catching the regular bus to Mark's house after school and then going home as if I was just getting off the after-school bus. We ended up having sex again except this time, I didn't feel weird afterwards.

A few weeks later, I spent the weekend at my friend's house. For some reason we started arguing, so I went to see Mark. As soon as he saw me, he took off running. I was heartbroken. I felt as if someone had stabbed me in the chest. Later that evening, my mother came to pick me up, and all I could think of was how Mark had run away from me. When we arrived home, I ran into my room and closed the door and cried. My mind kept racing for answers as to why he was running from me.

After crying thirty minutes nonstop, I looked into my top drawer and pulled out a razor. I was done feeling rejected. Crazy thoughts began to fill my mind. I kept thinking over and over how no one loves me. Voices in my head were telling me, "Cut yourself. You are an ugly Bigfoot." I grabbed the razor, held up my left wrist, and began to make deep cuts in my wrist. I begged God to take me away. I just wanted to be gone. I kept thinking how my mom never wanted me and now my first boyfriend had rejected me. I ended up with cuts on both of my arms, inside and out. Whatever I was feeling stayed over me for a while, and eventually I cried myself to sleep. The next morning, I put on a hoodie to cover myself as I left for school.

At school, I ended up talking to my close friends about my suicide attempt and I showed her my cuts. Unbeknownst to me, she told my teacher that I cut myself. My teacher told the guidance counselor, and the guidance counselor called my parents. When my parents came up to the school, they were livid. I was mad at my friend for opening her big mouth and telling. After the suicide attempt, I was referred to a psychiatrist for therapy sessions. It was just me and the therapist. The psychiatrist was always taking notes, but he was asking questions and telling me ways to handle my problems. I held back a lot because my psychiatrist was much older than me.

One day at my session, I was being nosey and looked at my paperwork. My paperwork stated that I was diagnosed with chronic depression. I guess after talking to him about how I felt that my mother didn't want me and the pain I was feeling deep down inside, I was not surprised. I was sad to my core. I could feel the pain, and it hurt.

Therapy was the first time in a while in which I felt that I was being heard and understood, but it wasn't enough to help me focus. My freshman year was the longest year ever. I was miserable by the end of it. The most memorable moment of my freshman year was meeting my two best friends, Jamelia and Brittany. They were amazing and very different.

Suicide

The Product of Depression

Until now, I have never spoken about my suicide encounter, but now it's time. My silence is broken, and the light of God shines brightly on an area of my life that was darkened by silence.

At age 16, I tried to end my life. I thought suicide would solve it all. I wanted it all to end the bullying and the rejection. One day when depression gripped my soul, I grabbed a razor and cut my wrists to stop the pain. I was tired of living a life full of questions that no one could answer or explain. When my suicide attempt failed, I thought, "Will I be mentally scarred for life?"

Eight short years later, I have two children and am no longer alone. No longer will I accept it's not okay to be me. I just want to live this life through to the end. Suicide could have taken me away that day because I couldn't bear the pain. I just wanted to be loved, not forgotten.

I have learned to accept myself for who I am. My story of bullying and rejection remains the same, but my failed suicide attempt has taught me that the game of life has so much to offer.

My number one goal is to show the people who counted me out that they were wrong. Suicide almost took a mother and a friend. What I couldn't see back then was that suicide isn't worth it. If you are wrestling with depression and suicide, you don't have to end it all, you can live. Life does get better, if you remain strong.

I will dedicate my life to show those who have attempted suicide and those that are contemplating suicide that their lives have purpose and that God has a beautiful legacy for them to fulfill.

4

Soccer and Reality Checks

10th Grade

I survived my first year of high school. Despite all the trials and tribulations, I got through it; boy, was I glad! I decided that this year would be different. I wasn't going to focus on boys, I was going to do my work and stay focused.

When soccer tryouts were announced, I decided to try out. To my surprise, I made the team. I don't know anything about soccer I thought, I don't even know what you do in this sport. However, I was willing to try something new. My number was 13. I picked the number 13 because it was my shoe size. I figured what a perfect match.

Soccer was a great sport. One day at one of our games, while I was on the field, I noticed a tall, dark, and handsome boy with a very nice smile. I also noticed that he could dress. A few weeks went by, and I kept seeing his face in the crowd. Because I was so focused on myself, I decided not to say anything to him. And besides, I didn't want to be rejected by someone new.

School was going good; I was passing all my classes. I loved my life for the first time. Finally, something good had my attention. Mason, the boy from the game, eventually approached me. We exchanged numbers and ultimately he became my boyfriend. We hung out at the soccer games. He "had jokes" and could always make me smile. Mason was a foster child like myself so we had a lot in common. We talked on the phone non-stop it seemed, and after some time, we ended up having sex. After a while my relationship with Mason fell apart, and I got back to reality.

5

Life Turns Upside Down

11th Grade

This chapter is written in loving memory of Mrs. Diann Jones Skinner

Mrs. Skinner,

What would I have done at A.R. Johnson High School without you? You encouraged me to remain on the correct path. You constantly told me that I would make it. I am so grateful to have met you. Until we meet again, continue to rest in peace. Thank you for believing in me.

After my relationship with Mason was over, I was determined to work harder in school to increase my GPA and figure out my plans for life after high school. My best friend in the entire world, Brittany, and I became closer than ever. Our schedules were similar; first period class was US History, and our teacher was Mrs. Skinner. Mrs. Skinner often threatened to give us an "F" and fail us, but she never did.

I began to drift my attention towards other things. I wanted to have some money in my pocket, so my niece (yes, my niece through my adopted family) helped me to get my very first job at Firehouse Subs. I was so excited to be earning my own money.

I still had no clue what I really wanted to do after high school, so I decided it would be best for me to join the military where I could make plenty of money. That was my plan and I was sticking to it.

One day while waiting for the bus, I met this little guy who was in the ninth grade. He asked me for my telephone number. I took his number because I was not allowed to have guys calling the house. When I got home that night I called him. His soft, nervous voice gave me a small giggle. We talked every day. One day when we were talking, I heard a guy with a deep, sexy, grown-sounding voice in the background. I asked, "Who is that?" He passed the phone to the guy I heard in the background, and we began to talk. His name was Jody. He sounded nice and had a mature, deeper voice than his brother.

Jody was nineteen and I was sixteen. I never stopped to think about the age difference because I was too excited that someone older was interested in me. I eventually started dating Jody; I was happy. I started skipping school, sneaking out late at night, sneaking him in the house, or walking thirty minutes in the middle of the night just to be with him. I was in love with him. The first time we had sex, I felt so special. He constantly told me how special I was, and I believed him. After a few weeks of dating, I started to feel sick. My body began to feel weird, so I stole a pregnancy test from the store.

The test was positive. The next day, my best friend skipped school with me to go with me to the Health Department. The test was again positive. I was pregnant at 16. My first thought was, "How am I going to explain this to my parents?" My friend Brittany consoled me and assured me that I was going to get through the pregnancy.

I returned to school after my visit to the Health Department with my mind on overload. I was nervous about where my life would go from that moment. I was going to be a mother and did not know how I was going to provide for my child. Despite the uncertainty on how things would turn out, I was excited. My heart was happy. I finally had someone to love me and I could love without limits.

My classmates began to find out quickly about my "little secret" the news spread like wildfire. Jody was very happy about the baby and proposed to me in the park with no ring. I still said, "yes"! I was sixteen, pregnant, and engaged to the first man to show me love.

Since the news was spreading around school, Mrs. Skinner found out. She asked me in the middle of the class, when I walked in late, if I was pregnant. I nodded in shame and excitement, "Yes." She asked me if my parents were aware and I replied, "No, I haven't told them." She told me that she was going to tell Mrs. Jones and she would call your parents. Afterwards, she marched me straight from her classroom to the office. Mrs. Jones, my church member, looked at me with a sour look when Mrs. Skinner said, "Shaena is pregnant." I saw the disappointment on her face.

Mrs. Jones had watched me grow up singing in the choir at church. When Mrs. Skinner left, Mrs. Jones asked me, "Are you really pregnant?" I replied, "Yes ma'am." Mrs. Jones told me that she had to call my parents and tell them. She asked me for the number, and my heart sank. I was terrified and a nervous wreck as she dialed the number. When someone answered the phone at home, Mrs. Jones said, "May I speak to Mrs. Ophelia Brinson?" It was Mom who answered the phone. Mrs. Jones said, "This is Mrs. Jones from A. R. Johnson High School. I am calling because I have Shaena in my office, and she has just informed me that she is pregnant." After the announcement, she handed the phone to me. My mother said, "Shaena, you're pregnant?" I replied, "Yes ma'am." She told me that we were going to talk when I got home from school. I hung the phone up and headed back to class.

I saw Mrs. Skinner in the hall as I headed to class. She stopped to tell me how my life was going to change. She told me that she believed in me and that everything would be okay. I began to cry, so she told Brittany to come out of class and check on me. When Brittany saw me, she asked, "What happened?" I said, "I am sure that I am going to die when I get home." Brittany told me that things would be okay.

When I arrived home I was tired. I tried my best to avoid Mom. I knew I had made a huge mistake at this point. I was about to bring another mouth to feed into her house. Mom was always reminding my sister and me that she would not take care of a baby for us; it would be our responsibility. Before my father was able to make it home, I called my sister and told her to come pick me up because I was about to run away. She told me that her boyfriend would be there in ten minutes, so I gathered my belongings. As I walked out the door, my father was coming down the road. He said, "Get your ass back to the house." Right away, I refused and continued to walk away from my neighborhood. My sister's boyfriend soon arrived. I moved in with my sister, and she was happy to have me.

It wasn't long before morning sickness kicked in. Often, I was too sick to get out of bed so I missed a great deal of school. Some days, I arrived so late that it was ridiculous. I was really struggling to maintain my grades, work, and deal with my pregnancy. I was determined to get through this. My relationship with Jody was getting rocky, and I was losing my mind worrying about the baby and how I would provide for my child. I thought that my fiancé would have answers to my questions but he didn't. Jody did not have a job. I was stressed out trying to explain to him how important it was that he get a job. Jody had no drive and it drove me insane. I was constantly cursing him out and hanging up the phone on him when I called him from work.

Greg, one of my best friends, always told me that no matter what I was experiencing, Jody and I were getting closer. I could talk to him about anything, and that was a positive thing because I was going through so much. When the day came for my first doctor's appointment, I told Jody not to come because I felt that he didn't care. I invited my best friend, Brittany, because she and I were closer.

I walked from my sister's house to the hospital. Brittany met me there moments before the nurse called me back to perform an ultrasound.

During the ultrasound, I lay there looking at the screen. When I saw my tiny baby, I smiled. The nurse didn't say anything to me during the ultrasound. When I was finished, I asked the nurse to bring Brittany back while I waited for the doctor. It seemed as if we sat for an hour before I saw the doctor. Finally, a knock at the door, and the doctor walked in to show me photos of my baby. He said, "There was no heartbeat. This is what we call a miscarriage." I burst into tears. My baby was dead inside me; I was heartbroken.

When I arrived home, I called Jody to tell him that I lost the baby. He was heartbroken. I felt terrible that I had not allowed him to be at the appointment. He came with me to the hospital the next day for my surgery. I called my parents and told them about the miscarriage and the surgery I needed the next day.

Jody was very supportive while we were at the hospital. Before I fell asleep, he kissed my forehead and held my hand. As they were pushing me to the operating room, I dozed off to sleep. When I awoke, I was back in the room with Jody. While he was holding my hand, I looked around and began to cry. I returned to my sister's house after the surgery. My mom bought some snacks by the house, and my oldest sister came to see me. My sister commented, "Maybe you don't need a baby right now." I went upstairs and locked myself in my room and cried all night.

Days later, I returned to school. The Guidance Counselor called me into her office and told me that I could not miss any more days of school. She said, "At the rate you're going, you are not going to pass the Georgia high school graduation test." On my way home from school that day, I had a lot on my mind. I decided to go by Brittany's house to talk, but she wasn't home. My walk home was long. When night time came, I went to my room. As I was dozing off to sleep, I heard my sister scream. I jumped out of bed and ran to see what was happening. I thought the screams were the result of an argument between my sister and her boyfriend.

When I got into the hallway heading towards the scream, a guy with a gun in his hand yelled, "Where is the money?" I was puzzled and afraid. He forced me downstairs with the gun pointed to my head and told me to lie on the living room floor. The gunman disappeared back upstairs. I thought about running to get help but I was terrified. I also did not want to leave my sister and nephew behind. The gunman kept asking for money, but we didn't have any. He became furious, came downstairs, and snatched me up from the floor, forcing me back upstairs, holding a sawed-off shotgun to my head.

He continued to demand money, and we kept explaining to him that we didn't have any. I was horrified at what was coming next when Willie, a family friend, pushed me out of his grip. The gunman took one step backwards, turned, and fired twice in Willie's direction. I actually saw the bullets fly through the air; I couldn't believe it. The gunman ran for the door after he fired his gun. I could hear Willie's mom screaming, as she ran towards the apartment. That night was very scary; I could have died. I spent the night at the hospital with Willie. His mother blamed me for her son getting shot because the bullet was for me. She believed that I was having sex with her son, and that is why he came to my rescue. Honestly, I was not having sex with Willie.

When I returned to school, the Guidance Counselor told me that I couldn't miss any more days of school if I wanted to graduate. I handed her the newspaper article about the shooting incident so that she could understand why I was not at school, but she showed no sympathy for what I had gone through.

Mrs. Jones called me in for a conference. She told me, "Your grades are low, and you will be placed on academic probation." I was allowed to stay in school, but I needed to bring up my grades. By this time, I wasn't up for the challenge. I asked her if I could transfer back to my zone school. She replied, "If you are sure you want to do that and get your parents' approval, you can return to your zone school." My parents gave their permission to leave A. R. Johnson High School.

I received my transfer paperwork and took them to my teachers for their signature. As I took my papers around to my teachers, Brittany begged me to stay. She said that she would help me. She didn't get how I felt and why I couldn't stay. I had almost lost my life, and I had lost my baby. I was lost and confused. I just needed a change, and a change indeed was coming.

I moved back in with my parents and broke up with Jody. I really needed to figure out my plans for my future. The following week, I arrived at my zone school. I was excited to be a new student. My Health teacher was a member of my church. He asked, "Why did you leave A. R. Johnson High School?" I told him that I had too much going on in my life. He welcomed me with open arms.

I met my next boyfriend in Health class. He was cool and very friendly. We were always together, and he didn't mind being seen with me. I enjoyed our relationship until one day I saw his friend Marcus. He grinned at me, and I thought he was so handsome. Later on, I saw Marcus again at soccer practice. He asked for my number, and with no regrets, I gave it to him. Marcus and I started talking and texting a lot. I still had a boyfriend but didn't care. After some time, I ended up having sex with Marcus. I thought nothing of it, but my boyfriend found out about it and confronted me in class in front of everyone. I was embarrassed so I lied and said, "No, I didn't sleep with Marcus." He pulled out his phone and showed me forwarded text messages that I had sent to Marcus. I was livid!

After all the drama with my boyfriend, I got over it fast because I had Marcus. He didn't want anyone to know about our relationship. One time he got mad at me for putting "S and M" as my text message signature and made me change it. After a while, I started hearing all kind of crazy things about Marcus. I heard that he was having sex with different girls at school. It upset me but I never said anything to him about it because I really did like Marcus. I just knew he was the one for me.

When prom came, Marcus ended up bringing another girl, and I came alone. I was angry. I couldn't understand why he came to the prom with another female when I was supposed to be his girlfriend. I pulled Marcus to the side and talked with him about his date. I wanted to know who she was and why she was there with him. I ended up going straight home after the prom. I was so over Marcus and his crazy ways; I broke up with him.

I no longer focused on Marcus and begin focusing on myself. A short time later, I met a guy named John. He was over six feet tall and a real sweetheart. He made me his girlfriend, but we did not date long because the things that he heard about me caused him to move away from me. I was no longer his girlfriend, but we remained very good friends. John was different; he didn't treat me like everyone else. He didn't judge me. I was free to be myself around him and it felt wonderful. His sense of humor made me even more attracted to him because we could joke and laugh with each other on any day at any time. My classmates did show a little jealousy over our relationship. We were both tall. We walked the halls together, goofing off and just having fun.

The school year was ending soon so I began to focus on my grades to make sure that I would be promoted to a senior. The hard work paid off, I was promoted.

6

A Role Model - Coach Tolbert

On September 17, 2016, God called home a true warrior, Coach Tolbert. Man, what I would do to give him one last hug! I want to dedicate this chapter in loving memory of Coach Tolbert.

Every Sunday, I sat in Calvary Church, looking to the right side of the church, checking to see if he was there so I could give him a hug. I've always had silent admiration for who he was as a man and a coach.

Coach Tolbert saw me through one of the roughest times of my life. He didn't judge me but helped me to stay strong and carry my head high.

I remember the first day I returned to my zone school, Glenn Hills High School. He wanted to know why I left A. R. Johnson High School, but I couldn't answer because I was so lost.

God has done some true work in my life, and I am sharing my story to help shape, mold, and change the lives of other young women.

Coach Tolbert would undoubtedly be surprised to know that I am writing a book. I had plans to tell him, but God had other plans. I have struggled to get to this place where I am able to complete the next two chapters of this book, but I know that the perfect time to do it is NOW.

I will miss him so very much. I pray one day that his family, friends, coworkers, and all the former students that he had the opportunity to leave his legacy with will have God's highest form of peace.

Ashlee, thank you for listening when I told you about the book. I know that God has you wrapped in his arms. May you forever be graced by God's love.

All my love, a former lost girl - Queen J

7

Senior Year: Pregnancy And Rejection

12th Grade

Marcus and I were girlfriend and boyfriend again. I got over the fact that he brought another girl to the prom, and I took him back.

It was summer, and I was so excited because Marcus and I were going on a trip together with the church. It was the church's annual children and youth trip to Carowinds Amusement Park. I worked extra hard so that I could pay for his ticket. I was giving Marcus money from my checks and making sure he was getting everything he wanted from me. When the time came, we went on our trip together, and we had so much fun.

I was enjoying life again when I began to feel weird. I decided to take a pregnancy test; it was negative. I believed that I was pregnant, so I took about three more tests. The tests were all negative. Now, I knew something wasn't right so I decided to go to the Health Department. The test at the Health Department confirmed that I was pregnant. I cried all day after hearing the test results.

When I called Marcus to tell him about the pregnancy, he insisted that the baby was not his because he believed that I was cheating on him. I was so confused because I was doing everything for Marcus, and I was baffled that he thought I was cheating on him; it made no sense to me.

During the summer break, I shared my pregnancy news with only a few people. When I got back to school, so many people knew about my pregnancy, and they were confronting Marcus. I was disappointed with myself because I had opened by big mouth about my pregnancy. Marcus denied that he was the father and never cared to speak to me. I walked around the school pregnant, and he ignored me.

John found me one day by my locker. He needed a place to put his books so I agreed to share my locker with him. He reminded me to keep my head up and not to worry about what anyone thought.

It was hard going to school every day and seeing Marcus. We had classes together, and yet he still refused to speak to me on any level. I was embarrassed and hurt. I was always alone. My father always took me to my doctors' appointments and dropped me off. I texted my doctor appointments to Marcus, but he never showed up.

I needed someone to talk to so I went to my old health teacher and told him about my situation. I remember as if it happened yesterday, the look on his face when I told him that I was pregnant. To my surprise, not once did he put me down or count me out. He joked with me and supported me through the entire process. Man, until this day, I love that man. Whenever I saw him I always gave him the biggest hug because truly, I do not know where I would be without him.

I missed a lot of days from school due to my doctor appointments, sleeping all day, or just suffering with depression from not having Marcus's support. My teachers gave me my class assignments and helped me to stay encouraged.

I met Keisha during this time. She was pregnant, and her child's father was incarcerated. We became very close, and it appeared that nothing could tear us apart. We did everything together, and our babies were due around the same time. Thinking about her now makes me remember just how special she was to me. The times when I had no one else she was right there beside me, pregnant and wobbling down the hall with me. She wanted a boy and I wanted a girl. In the end, we both ended up with the opposite sex.

I attempted to reach out to Marcus on numerous occasions. It was crazy how we were in one class together each day, and yet I hardly heard from him nor was I acknowledged by him. People often told me that he had "disowned" my child but through all of the drama I managed to stay strong and smile.

One day while we were sitting in math class, Marcus slipped me a note that said "Quanelias Zachariah Brown." A few nights later, I was arguing on the phone with Marcus, and my foster mother overheard me. When I got off the phone, she called me into her room and asked me, "Shaena, why are you arguing? You made your mistake so accept it and move on." I didn't understand why she wanted me to let it go. I was not ready and no one could convince me that it was time to move on.

John was like a light at the end of the tunnel. He came to my locker often, cracking jokes about how big I had gotten and telling me I was going to make it. I admired John from afar because surely we could never be together because I was pregnant by someone else. I was just glad that we were still tight after everything that had happened between us.

Marcus was harsh towards me. He would see me at school and purposely ignore me. I always wondered what I had done to deserve such behavior from him. I needed his support and yet he gave me nothing at all; no hello and no goodbye. He hardly ever answered the phone when I called. He responded to a text message one day and told me to come over to his place. Brittany picked me up and drove me to his house.

When we arrived, I knocked on the door. His mother came to the door and said, "Are you the girl that's supposed to be pregnant by Marcus?" I replied, "Yes." She then asked, "Why don't you leave him alone?" When I left, I called Marcus to find out why he asked me to come to his house. When he answered the phone, he was laughing. I asked him why he would do such a thing to me. Even Brittany was angry about the "come to my house" charade. I wondered if Marcus was the same guy I had bought clothes for and given money to. He just didn't seem the same. He was so selfish. I was pregnant and alone.

As I got closer to giving birth, I became more and more uncertain of what lay ahead. Before leaving school on maternity leave, I collected my assignments from my teachers. One of the assignments that stood out the most was from my Education teacher, Ms. Clark. Her assignment for me was to tell my story on how becoming a teen mother had affected my life: what was different with my life and how was I coping with it all. I was so excited about the assignment! It sparked my interest beyond my wildest dreams. For the very first time, I would be able to express everything that I was going through. The fact that Ms. Clark had come up with such a brilliant assignment was so awesome.

On March 6, 2009, three months before the end of my senior year, I gave birth to my 7lb. 13oz. son, Quanelias Zachariah Jones. Marcus wasn't there for me when I gave birth. He came to see me the night after I delivered our son and told me that I needed to trust him. Although my son's father was not there for me, I managed to make it through the hard part. When I completed my class assignment for Ms. Clark, I encompassed a great deal of the information about my pregnancy and what I had been through.

When my son was a few weeks old, I was given an invitation to Honors Day. I hadn't been to Honors Day since middle school. I was thinking to myself what had I done to go to Honors Day. I remember thinking to myself, after all the days that I had missed from school, why am I invited; it must be a mistake.

At Honors Day, I received the Education Award for having the highest average in Ms. Clark's class. I had done it! I had an award for something that I enjoyed doing. I was proud of myself. I had delivered a beautiful son and in a few weeks, I would be graduating. I earned the honor to graduate because I passed all of the Georgia High School Graduation tests.

8
Graduation 2009

With graduation right around the corner, I was super excited even though I had no clue as to what lay ahead for me after high school. I was excited because with the grace of God, I was about to beat one of those nasty statistics that say, "Girls who get pregnant in high school are likely to drop out." Not me, I was well on my way towards something bigger.

Attending graduation practice the last week of school instead of going to regular classes was a relief. I didn't have to get my son up so early. Quanelias was two months old, and I was eighteen and about to step into a new part of my life. Marcus' parents decided to keep our son for graduation. Since my parents were older, I felt it would be a little easier on his parents.

On the morning of graduation, I woke up feeling like a champion! When I arrived at the arena, I snapped a few photos with some friends before the ceremony began. Even though Marcus and I graduated together, we didn't speak to each other. In a way, I was not surprised. Perhaps Marcus blamed me for ruining his senior year.

As the music began to play, we marched from behind the curtain. Seeing the crowd, I began to feel the moment. I was emotional, high school was really over. The crowd was roaring and screaming our names. The atmosphere was filled with excitement. I was so nervous, anticipating hearing my name called, but when the announcer said, "Shaena A. Jones," my face lit up; I was proud to walk across the stage. I grabbed my diploma cover and walked off the stage. "I am done," I thought to myself. I could hear and see my family's excitement. After the ceremony was over, we marched behind the curtain to receive our diplomas.

I called Marcus so that I could see my son after graduation, but with people scattering everywhere, I was unable to see him, and that made me feel empty. To make matters worse, the envelope I received had a notice from the school saying that I owed money for books, and my diploma was being held. When I told my mother, she was so mad because she had paid the fines, and the school had made a mistake. It took about a week to get my diploma from the school; I was so excited. I made it!

It seemed as if I had gone from a church going girl to a single, teen mother overnight. My path was crowded; I had no direction. I stopped going to church because of the criticism.

I couldn't bear people looking down on me because I was a teenage mom. I guess my foster parents just didn't know how to cater for my needs and didn't take the time to understand what I was facing. I struggled with depression. My biological mother was not a consistent force in my life.

I allowed circumstances to distract me off course. I felt as if all of my dreams had died, so I decided to join the military. I didn't know how to make a difference in my life. I didn't know what would make me happy. The only certainty was the reality that I had to take care of my child. I was making so many sacrifices. I was a true definition of a single mother struggling to make it on her own. I constantly told myself that I wanted to make a difference in the lives of others. I never want anyone to feel the way that I felt lost.

I believed that I could do anything that I put my mind to do, but what was it that I truly wanted to accomplish? It seemed for a moment that everything I put my hands on fell apart. All of the things that were happening in my life wasn't who I was destined to become. They were lessons for the person I was destined to become. So here I am now, many years later, sharing my story with you, a young Queen. I have a story that needs to be heard.

I have gone through so much in life and have come out, so I know that you can make it regardless of what you face in life. It doesn't matter if you have a father or not; you can and will overcome your negative circumstances because you are the daughter of a king. Believe it – don't sell yourself short!

9

Letters That Explain It All

Dear Mom,

I have always loved you despite all the pain that I have faced through the years. I've sat at my window day after day, awaiting your return. I just knew one day that you would come and pick me up. However, that didn't happen; you never showed up. I cried constantly, wondering why I was never enough for you to love me. Why didn't you want your daughter? For so many years, all I wanted was you. I always pondered what it would be like to do mother-daughter activities. How amazing it would have been to have my own mom at Honors Day!

Mom, you have always meant the world to me, and no one or anything could ever change that. Spending time with you was something I would at times look forward to and others not so much. I don't know what happened to you as I got older. I'll never understand why you went away; you took a part of me with you. I remember so clearly the times I was dropped off and you were nowhere to be found, so many times, you would leave for days at a time.

I have looked for you in everything that I have laid my eyes on. I wanted to find you. I wanted to be loved, held, and needed by you. You will forever be my mom, and I will be your daughter. Thank you for giving me life. I love you forever Mom.

Your December 24th Girl,
Shaena

Dear Dad,

How is it possible for a man to abandon his own flesh and blood, his daughter, his princess? I needed you. I wanted you…I really wanted you and no one else. I was heartbroken. I needed you to tell me it would be okay and you were never there. I have loved you for so long and cried when I wasn't able to see you. Why didn't you come back for me? Why didn't you think to simply tell me that I was beautiful? Was I not enough?

You will always be a part of my life. I will never forget what you taught me through the way you have treated me: love myself first. Your daughter that has always loved you.

Your Queen,
Shaena

Dear Reader,

I was searching for my parents' love in others. I wanted to be loved. I gave my body away in exchange for love. There was a void in my heart that I wanted filled. For years, my life was upside down, and I never understood why I was experiencing so much pain inside. I did not know how to deal with rejection and pain.

One day, I decided to take steps towards self-healing. I started surrounding myself with people I thought could love me enough to help me forget. I did this at the expense of being used, mislead, and unappreciated. All I ever wanted was love. No one took the time to tell me how beautiful I was, or what it meant to not have sex with a boy before marriage. Sure, I learned about sex in school through sex education. Sex education in school focused on sexually transmitted diseases. We never had meaningful conversations or guiding principles about sex.

If you haven't had a conversation with your parents about sex, and you feel as if you are ready for sex or thinking about it, please talk to them. They will greatly appreciate your honesty. Parents, please take the time to explain sex to your children. I can't stress the importance of doing this. I learned so much about the world and people when I was seeking love. I could not control the way others treated me; however, I learned that self-love is the most important thing you can give to yourself. No one can take that from you.

When you take your focus away from the things that matter in life, the harder it will be to get caught up. The biggest lesson I learned is that my body is special and allowing myself to give it to people in search of love was not smart. I should have asked for help and been more open to receive it. I believe, regardless of where your path has taken you, that you can choose to make better decisions. You can rise above peer pressure. You can be the one to make a difference in the lives of others.

I am the girl who struggled to make it. I was left unheard and alone. I dealt with my problems the best way I could. Now that I am older and looking back, I want to encourage some young lady reading this book to be wise. Life is full of twists, cheers, tears, ups and downs, and if you aren't careful, you will find yourself in difficult circumstances you never imagined.

The songwriter wrote: "Hold onto your innocence. Use your common sense. You're worth waiting for, be strong, don't give in, blessings come with patience, until we meet again, I'm praying for you."

Dear God,

Use this story to transform the lives of my little sisters everywhere. Help them to be strong in all they do. Encourage them when they feel weak. Keep their mind focused on those things that are good and will help them to grow and reach their full potential. Increase them, fill them with happiness, joy, peace, love, and light. Help them to know who they are and that no matter what someone else says, they are enough.

Help my fatherless sisters have a healing piece of You so that they will never feel lonely or void of the love of a man. I pray they have Your love from within. God, touch the hearts and minds of my motherless sisters. I know the pain they feel, it runs deep. Help them to pick themselves back up when they are down. There is something about the love of a mother. You said that You would be a mother to the motherless. Restore peace and hope that will give them inner strength. Help my sisters to rise up and move mountains.

I decree and declare that Your words shall not return to You void and everyone that reads my story will know that You allowed them to hear it at the perfect timing in their life. God, thank You in advance for what You have already done.

Your Daughter,
Queen J
Shaena

Personal Reflections Workbook

Let's Reevaluate 58

You Are A Young Queen..61

Every Action Has A Consequence 63

Speak Up, Speak Out 66

Involve Yourself...68

Learn Yourself 69

Attitude..71

Friends 72

Learn to Save Your Money.......................................73

Learning to Express Yourself....................................74

Goals, Dreams, & Faith..75

Keys to Life 78

Final Words..79

Let's Reevaluate

Now that you know my story, let's talk about you and what path you are headed down.

Where are you in life right now?

____

____

____

____

Do you believe that you are on a positive or negative path?

____

____

____

____

Why are you on that path?

____

____

____

____

What are your influences (people, places, or things)?

____

____

____

____

What is it that you really want to be and do?

____

____

____

____

____

What are you doing really well that is helping you get there?

____

____

____

____

____

What are you not doing well that is preventing you from getting there?

____

____

____

____

____

What will you do differently tomorrow to meet those challenges?

____

____

____

____

____

As you reflect on your answers, if you are not on a path headed towards success, no pressure. It's never too late to grow and change so that you are headed in the right direction. Don't stop now, keep reading, it gets better.

Of all the things, I could have understood as a young Queen, I find these to be the most important.

- You are a young Queen
- Every action has a consequence
- Speak up, speak out
- Involve yourself
- Attitude
- Friends
- Learn to save money early
- Learn to express yourself
- Learn yourself

I will teach you a little about each of the above and have you work through multiple exercises to help you fully understand the lesson.

You Are A Young Queen

You think if he calls you pretty, it will hide your scars of the real issues. You think because no one knows you've been beaten, abused, and stripped of your innocence that they don't care.

You may feel as though the bullying will never end so you react without thinking, wanting love, spreading your legs, allowing him to open your mind to another world in which your level of maturity can't even comprehend.

You may think that I'm speaking from a place where there is no way out or I could ever understand your struggle. It's not that I've been there or I've done that. The fact is, I can relate to what you are feeling: lost, confused, and trying to self-heal while searching for the love you deserve.

Someone should have taught you that you're simply beautiful because of who you are. Not for your curves or the way you feel inside but because you are really beautiful inside and out.

Grab your writing tool and let's get to work.

I AM	I AM NOT
Beautiful	Ugly
Smart	Dumb/Stupid
Productive	Barren
Confident	Doubtful
Energetic	Half-hearted
Worth being loved	Worthless
Brave	Cowardly
Young Queen	Peasant

______________________ is ______________________
______________________ is not ______________________

*Example: Shaena is <u>beautiful</u>. Shaena is not <u>Ugly</u>.

Can you think of words that describe who you are and who you are not.
Fill in the box below?

I AM	I AM NOT

Use the "I am" words on a daily basis.

_________________________________ is

_________________________________ is not

Example:

______is beautiful

______is smart

Beauty is not defined by what is on the outside but what is on the inside.
If you look inside yourself, you will discover the real beauty you have. In
the space below, write what makes you beautiful.

____

____

____

____

____

____

Every Action Has A Consequence

Each decision you make impacts your future. When I reflect on certain moments in my teenage years, I realize that each and every action had a consequence. Consequences can be defined as a result or effect of an action or condition.

If you are anything like me, I'm sure when you heard the word "consequences," you felt that you were in some type of trouble. The reality is, consequences come in two forms: good or bad.

Think of a time when you made a decision and it produced a negative consequence. For example: You didn't study for a test and failed the test, or lied to your mother to avoid the consequences, or you posted something inappropriate on the internet that resulted in losing the use of the computer.

Good consequences. You studied so you passed the test or you posted something appropriate on the internet and earned more computer time. Doing what is right will result in good consequences and possibly rewards.

In the blanks below, write the first things that came to your mind.

____

____

____

____

____

From the negative action written above, what are some steps you could have taken to produce a positive outcome?

____

____

____

____

____

Let's talk about the negative consequences of sex. For me, the decision to have unprotected sex after I lost my baby resulted in getting pregnant again. Having a baby was both a good and bad consequence. Good consequence because the baby was a blessing, but it was a bad decision because I had no financial means to provide for the child; I was a teenager in school.

List below what you believe are some consequences of teenage sex.

____

From your list above, how can you make a difference in your life to see positive results?

____

Did you know that sex can bring you more than a baby? Did you list the risk of catching a STD? Did you know that HIV and AIDS are spread through unprotected sex? As you reflect on your list above, ask yourself, "Do I want to continue my negative actions?"

Think of those around you that will be affected by the decisions you make (mother, father, siblings, friends, church, community, etc.). I am challenging you to change negative behaviors into positive behaviors. From your list above, how can you make a difference in your life to see positive results?

Please accept my challenge and sign the commitment to make a change.

(Your name) ____ has recognized that I have behaviors that I know will not produce positive consequences. I am committing to work towards changing those behaviors and alleviate reaping negative consequences.

(Hashtag your commitment to #Commited2Change #C2C.)

As you accept this challenge, stay committed to it. Don't give up and don't give in. Keep striving towards making wise decisions, and in the end, you will come out a winner. Had I thought out my actions, I would have paid more attention to what I was doing and would have been more careful. If you want different results, you have to do something different.

Fill in this page with your thoughts and feelings about what consequences mean to you and how making a change can impact your future.

Speak Up, Speak Out

As young women, a lot of times we experience things in life, and we can't understand them. Your solution for direction can be as simple as asking someone for guidance, advice, or help. We must be willing to lend a helping hand and avoid being quick to write off a teen girl who is misunderstood. Take her by the hand and guide her. Give her the ear you wish you had. Be open to our future generations. If one person had reached out to me, maybe they could have saved me.

As women, we must teach our daughters, nieces, cousins, and other teens around the world how to become better women. You may think they will not listen, but there is someone waiting to hear from you. Always remember that you don't have to be perfect, just willing to bless someone else because you have been where they are.

Don't be afraid or ashamed to speak to someone about your issues. It is important that you do not try to suppress your issues or place them on a back burner. Be bold and find someone you can trust to help you.

Fear is a mind thing. In order to overcome it, you have to stand up and be strong enough to overcome the thoughts that are trying to hold you back from accomplishing what you set out to do.

Reasons to Speak Up and Speak Out

You don't know as much as you think you know. You only know the things you've experienced. There is always someone who has been through what you are dealing with. Having someone to give you guidance can make a difference.

If you are not sure who you can talk to or where to start, below is a list of people that you can talk to about your problems.

- Your mother (Momma knows best…believe this)

- You father (You'll always be Daddy's little girl)

- Aunt (Who doesn't love having an aunt who spoils you?)

- Teacher (You spend 85 % of your week in school)

List three people you can call for advice. Add the phone number, email, and social media information beside each name.

1) ____

____

____

____

2) ____

____

____

____

3) ____

____

____

____

Involve Yourself

All around you there are opportunities for you to be involved in some type of activity such as sports, organizations, church, and you could even volunteer. It is important that you are involved in activities so that it can keep you busy.

Advantages of being involved are:

- Experience for your resume

- Meeting new people

- Helping others

Keep focused on the things that matter. Where your attention goes, energy flows.

If you have nothing to keep your attention, you can find a doorway to trouble.

What are some things you can do or get involved in?

____

____

____

____

____

____

____

____

____

____

____

____

Learn Yourself

Take time to learn yourself. Make you happy. If you are aware of yourself, then you will know how to make yourself happy when you face challenges. Learning myself has made me understand the importance of making myself happy above anyone else.

What is your favorite color? _______________________________________

What is your favorite food? _______________________________________

____

What's your dream job? ____

____

What is your dream career? ____

____

Who is your role model? ____

____

What makes you happy?____

____

____

What makes you sad? ____

____

____

Where is your happy place? ____

____

____

Do you go to your happy place often? If not, why not? _____________

____

____

____

Describe yourself below.

____

____

____

____

____

Now that you have described yourself, read what you wrote. Is this the best description of you?

Attitude

You can have the most beautiful face, the best work ethic, but the sad reality is, you will never get to where you want to be in life with a bad attitude. Your attitude can make the difference between someone reaching out to help you or not. It would be a bad thing if you needed a job, and your attitude prevented you from being chosen for the position.

What has caused you to have a bad attitude? Why do you chose to be angry? Does it benefit you to have a bad attitude?

To have a positive attitude requires you to be in control of your emotions and squash any flare-ups of a negative attitude. Try the exercises below.

How is your attitude? _______________________________________

____

____

If you have a poor attitude, how can you work on changing it? ______

____

____

____

Ways to help you have a positive attitude:

- Exercise

- Get plenty of sleep

- Learn something new

- Meditate and breathe deeply

- Be appreciative for all that you have

- Pray

Friends

The people that you choose to associate yourself with today, say a lot about where you will end up tomorrow. Just because we identify those close to us as friends, it does not mean that they are good for us.

Learn to love yourself enough to avoid those people who bring drama and negativity into your life. Stay focused; every decision you make impacts your future.

Who are your friends? (Choose this label carefully because they are a reflection of yourself.)_______________________________________

____

____

____

Why are you friends with the people you have listed above? _________

____

____

____

Are your friends like-minded? _________________________________

Do your friends bring drama into your life? _____________________

What type of things do you and your friends do together? _________

____

____

____

Are these activities beneficial to you? (If not, why are you doing them?)

____

____

____

____

Learn to Save Your Money

Ask your parents to help you open a bank account. Save every rusty penny you find, you are going to need it when you meet the real world. Your parents may be responsible for you now, but one day you will be on your own.

Do you know what it feels like to leave home with nothing but good advice? I do, and it's not a good feeling. It is sad when all of your money goes to bills, and you don't have any extra money. Even if you are planning to attend college, saving a few extra bucks for a rainy day is a good idea. Besides, if you have some money, you can avoid putting the full financial weight on your parents. Volunteer at home to do extra chores to earn money. Saving is an essential part of life. Save now or you will most definitely wish you had later.

Do you save your money? _______________________________________

Is saving important to you? _____________________________________

If you are not saving your money, will you start saving? ____________

____

____

Set a goal on how much money to save. (Example: Commit to saving two dollars a week.) _______________________________________

____

____

Can you save more than what you have listed above? ______________

____

____

____

____

Learning to Express Yourself

Self-expression is the expression of one's feelings, thoughts, or ideas, especially in writing, art, music, or dance.

The thought of self-expression is powerful. Just imagine that you are going through something and you know how to paint. You could paint an image and share it with your mentor (mom, sister, dad) and explain it. Can you imagine how much of a difference that would make in your life?

What are you good at doing? _________________________________

____

____

____

I am leaving space below for you to explore your creative side. If you write poetry, write. If you like to draw, draw. If you write music, drop your lyrics. Whatever you do, execute it to the fullest of your ability and never allow someone to take it from you.

Goals, Dreams, & Faith

A goal is the object of a person's ambition or effort; an aim or desired result.

What are your goals? ______________________________________

____

____

____

____

____

Dreams are imaginary and they don't produce tangible results without faith. You need goals to make your dreams real.

What do you dream of becoming? ___________________________

____

____

____

____

Do you have faith that your dreams will come true? If not, then they may not come true. ______________________________________

Faith is complete trust or confidence in someone or something. Now that you have written your goals, create a plan that includes the steps you need to take to achieve them. Work with a teacher, parent, or mentor to help you formulate tangible steps to achieve your goals.

Are you familiar with a vision board? If not, I suggest that you get one. A vision board is like a road map. On a vision board, you can post a variety of things such as your goals, words that you live by, places you wish to visit, and the things in life you want or desire to obtain. The vision board only works if you believe in it.

A list of things you will need to create your vision board are: one poster board (any color), markers, magazines, or photos of the things that describe your goals, glue, and your creativity.

Start by decorating your board any way you like. Even if you want more than the materials I listed above, it's your board; go for it. Next, hang your vision board where you can see it and make sure you look at it daily. I have several vision boards because as you grow, your vision changes. Don't be afraid to take the old one down and make a new one.

If you don't like the vision board, some alternative ideas are: Start a dream book, using a three ring binder decorated however you want, and fill it with your thoughts, ideas, visions, dreams, and self-expressions. Keep a daily journal with your thoughts, feelings, observations, experiences, etc.

My time with you is done, but before I go, it's <u>your time</u> for you to write <u>your story</u>!

Keys to Life

Here is a list of things that I wish I had known and understood.

- Life goes on beyond middle and high school.

- You are more than a conqueror.

- You have to use your mind.

- Look in the mirror and remember you are beautiful.

- My life is great.

- Everything works together for your highest good.

- Pray (doesn't have to be a fancy prayer).

- Ask God to help me and show me where I need to be.

- I am a young Queen

What are some life keys that you have learned along the way?

____

____

____

____

____

____

____

____

____

____

____

____

Final Words

Knowledge is not power; applied knowledge is power. Take this book with you as you grow and remember the lessons you have learned.

Before I go, I pray that you have learned more than just a little from "The Journal of My Journey." You are about to go back into the world a better young Queen.

I have faith that my story has inspired you to pursue excellence. I pray that you have found what you needed as you read the pages of this book. I believe that no matter where you go from here, you will be an amazing Queen.

I was once where you are
I was once lost and confused
I felt trapped inside
I pursued what I thought was love
It is my life passion to "Go Be Great"
Shaena

"I know the plans I have for you says the lord, plans to prosper you and not to harm you plans to give you hope and a future." Jeremiah 29: 11

God has done some amazing work in my life and I pray He continues to guide my path towards His higher calling on my life.

To my mother and father, Mr. & Mrs. Frank and Ophelia Brinson, you are my heroes! If God had not graced you with the strength to be my angels, I would not be where I am right now in my life. You will always be my *guardian angels*. Every day I think of you and I am forever grateful!